my little life

When I Won a Prize

Look out for more *My Little Life* titles:

When Ellie Cheated
When Scott Got Lost
When Geri and I Fell Out
When Dad Went on a Date
When Shah Went Weird

And you can write to Tiff by e-mail at:
tiffany.little@hodder.co.uk

Jenny Oldfield

my little life

When I Won a Prize

illustrated by Martina Farrow

Hodder
Children's
Books

a division of Hodder Headline Limited

A Catalogue record for this book is available from the British Library

ISBN 0 340 85076 0

Printed and bound in Great Britain by
Bookmarque Ltd, Croydon, Surrey

The paper and board used in this paperback by
Hodder Children's Books are natural recyclable products
made from wood grown in sustainable forests.
The manufacturing processes conform to the environmental
regulations of the country of origin.

Hodder Children's Books
A division of Hodder Headline Limited
338 Euston Road, London NW1 3BH

A big thank you to the hundreds of kids I met
on school visits who helped me with ideas
for these books!

Monday, April 1st

Your stars – *Like most Leos, you're not shy when it comes to boys. Maybe you'll be first in your class to have a smooch!*

I'm planning to ignore that.

The day got off to a lousy start with big bro Scott's idea of a joke. He put fake soap in the bathroom that turns your skin bright blue. I fumbled my way to the sink, splooshed some water on to my face and rubbed in the soap. Then I looked in the mirror – Waaagh!

Scott stands at the door yelling, 'April Fool!'

How childish is that! I mean, he's fifteen years old! The last time I did an April Fool was four years ago, when I was seven and I put a live worm in Mum and Dad's bed. Well, it was alive when I put it in, but it was pretty squidged when it came out, poor thing.

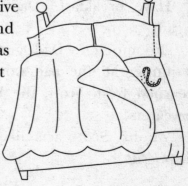

Now I have a massive guilt attack every time I see one – I realize that worms have rights, just like everything else in this world.

'Look at me! I can't go to school like this!' I wail, staring at my blue face.

It's karma – the worm kingdom is fighting back!

'April Fool!!' Scott croaks until he cracks up.

Fifteen years old and he still gets a buzz out of tormenting me.

'It won't come off!' I'm scrubbing like mad when Dad wanders in. 'Look at me! This is what Scott did!'

'Yeah, he got me too. Don't worry, it does come off with plenty of warm water.'

'I'm not going to school if it doesn't!' Eventually, the dye begins to fade. Now I'm only a fetching shade of pale blue.

'Have breakfast,' Dad suggests. 'Then try again.'

The moment Dad goes back downstairs, I mutter all the bad words I know, which I learned from Scott, the World Champion of Swearers.

'Wooh!' Scott acts like he's shocked, the hypocrite.

(hypocrisy/hi-pok'ri-si/n. simulation of virtue, insincerity

hypocrite/hip'ə-krit/n. person guilty of hypocrisy)

It's my fave word.

Anyhow, in the end I went to school feeling like I'd rubbed a cheese grater over my face. But at least I was the right colour. Kind of.

'Hey, how come you look so red?' Chucky Gilbert asked me.

(Is this the kind of kid I'm supposed to smooch? I don't think so!) 'Get lost, Chucky!'

I rushed to join Ellie, Shah and Geri.

'Guess what? Ellie's had a major row with Lisa Sharman and Carli Hewitt!' Geri reported, while Shah put her arm round Ellie's shoulder and Ellie snivelled big time.

'What kind of row?' The news was obviously just breaking. There was a gang of girls around Carli and Lisa at the far side of the cloakroom.

'About Gemini,' Geri explained. 'They had a band rehearsal last night and Miss Westlake made Ellie lead singer, ahead of Carli and Lisa.'

'Boo-hoo!' Ellie gave the sobs everything she'd got. 'It wasn't my fault!'

Shah soothed her troubled spirit. 'Forget it. It's their problem, not yours.'

I picked up the strong whiff of jealousy in the wind. Drawing Geri to one side, I asked what Carli and Lisa had done to make Ellie cry.

'Lisa called her a rich bitch. She said everyone knew Miss Westlake had only chosen her because her dad gives oodles of cash to the PTA!'

Ouch! It's true; the Shelbourns are rolling in money. True again that Ellie gets given everything she wants, clotheswise, and her bedroom is stuffed with tellys, computers and music systems. On top of which, Ellie is a total babe – long, blonde hair, fashion model material. Other kids are bound to be jealous. Even me, deep down, and I've been her friend since Reception Class!

Geri whispered the rest of the argument. 'After Lisa had said the rich bitch thing, Carli came in with the fact that in any case, Ellie couldn't sing!'

Double-ouch! Actually, Ellie *had* taken singing lessons to get into Gemini. OK, so she'd faked one of the early auditions, but then she'd worked really hard and now she deserved the top slot. 'And this is what they're spreading around?' I asked Geri.

'Boo-hoo!' Ellie wailed.

The gaggle of girls across the room oohed and aahed at Lisa and Carli's version.

Geri nodded. 'I'd have told them to naff off.'

'Yeah, but Ellie's the sensitive type. She looks dead confident, but underneath, she needs everyone to like her. She hates it when people get at her.'

Geri's eyes widened. 'Woah, Tiff, what're you on about?'

Ask Geri who won the Ladies' Singles at Wimbledon in 1992, and she'll reel it off in a nano-second. But if you want to look into reasons why people act the way they do, forget it! That's how come Geri wants to play hockey for England and I want to be a mega famous writer.

'C'mon,' I said, making my way back to Shah and Ellie.

'Listen!' I told Ellie. 'Carli and Lisa can say what they like, everyone knows Miss Westlake doesn't have favourites. Which means she must have chosen you because you're the best dancer and singer in the band.'

'Thanks, Tiff,' Ellie sniffed. 'I guess I shouldn't let them upset me.'

Ellie crying looks like anyone else; she gets the red, puffy eyes and the blotchy skin.

'Hey, it's the price of fame!' Shah teased. 'Get used to it!'

The Price of Fame. I made this the title of the timed essay we had to write in English.

'I want you to write a reasoned, logical argument about a subject of your own choosing,' Gorgeous George explained.

The class sighed. Squealer and Callum groaned out loud.

Mr Fox took no notice. 'This isn't you being creative, this is you being analytical. We call this style of writing discursive, and it's a major part of your coursework when it comes to GCSE.'

More groans and sighs. But I'm already thinking, Great! I can write about what happens to people when they get mega rich and famous. How they get mobbed by fans and journalists every time they leave the house. How they lose their privacy, and everybody wants a little piece of them. How other people are jealous and start getting bitchy. And you don't even have to be a movie star for this to happen. Look at Princess Di.

'OK, so let's have some examples of subjects you might choose to write about,' George went on. 'Adam, what d'you think?'

Squealer squirmed and went red. 'Dunno, sir.'

'Well, what topics interest you? What really gets you going?'

'Girls!' Chucky sniggered.

Excuse for major outburst among the boys.

Georgeous turned it around. 'Right, so Adam might write an essay called, "The Effect of Raging Hormones on Pre-Teenage Boys"!'

This time it was the girls who laughed.

'Fuchsia, what about you?' George turned to someone with more than half a brain.

Shah blushed. 'Maybe something about half-sisters?'

Which she knows plenty about. Her half-sister, Skye, is coming down from Scotland this Easter for a visit. Shah didn't even know about Skye until last Christmas, but it turns out they get on great (see diary entries for December and January).

'Good,' George agreed. He told us we needed a proper introduction and conclusion.

'Convince me that your argument is right. Really make me believe what you say.'

The Price of Fame
by Tiffany Little

Most people, when they look at celebrities on TV and read about them in Hello! magazine, wish that they too could be famous.

They think about the money they would have, and the way everyone would recognize them. They would sign autographs and have their picture taken every time they stepped out of the door. The best seats in any restaurant would be reserved.

These are the perks of fame, but what about the price you would have to pay?

For instance, imagine the jealousy that people would feel against you. Old friends, who knew you before you were famous, might wonder why you should suddenly have so much money and attention. They might start stories behind your back, and the gossip would soon be splashed across the pages of OK! Then you would wonder

14

whether these people had ever been real friends.

A second big problem about fame is to do with new friends. Lots of people would flatter you and say how great you were, but would you really be able to believe them? Might they be hypocrites, just saying these things so that they could become ~~hanger-ons~~ hangers-on? Would you ever be able to trust them and tell them about important things? Remember, that journalist from Hello! is waiting just around the corner!

Another difficulty surrounding fame is the begging letters you would receive. Would it be true that a mother who writes to you really does need £5,000 for an operation on her son's paralysed legs? How would you prove it? And how bad would you feel if you turned her down?

Then there's the fact that you could never go out without your make-up, or dressed in smart clothes. Plus, you'd always be worried about the future. Will you be as famous next year as you are this year? How will it feel to be a has-been, washed up and with nobody caring? In this way, fame could be like a drug; a habit which is hard to kick.

So you see, there are at least as many problems to do with being famous as there are advantages. In my mind though, if I had to choose, I still think the temptation to be famous is strong. Who can resist the pull of being popular and successful? Not me, for one.

But I would go into it with my eyes open, knowing that there is a price to be paid, and doing my best to keep my feet on the ground. The key would be to hang on to family and friends, and never to think that deep down you are more important than anyone else.

I wrote this in forty minutes at home. George trusts us not to cheat on the timing. I think it's OK, except the ending got a bit rushed.

Squealer called me a freak after English today. He said he caught me smiling during the lesson, when everyone else was moaning and groaning.

Adam Pigg called *me* a freak!!!

Tuesday, April 2nd

Your stars – *He's not the cutest boy in school, but he's funny, caring and a good mate. Never mind what people say, you and he could be perfect together!*

I'm gonna change my mag, I really am!

Ellie cheered up a bit today. Carli and Lisa are still being mean, but a lot of kids came up and told her she made Gemini what it was. Without her, the band would be nothing. This did her a lot of good.

I handed my essay in.

Shah got told off by Mr (Maths teacher) White. Again!

Geri's been picked for next term's junior tennis team, so she was whacking a ball against a wall during the whole of lunch-break.

Only one more day of school before we break up for Easter.

Got home and e-mailed a fan letter to Charlotte Irvine:

Hi, Charlotte!

I want to let you know how much I enjoyed your latest book, Tigers in the Dust. I've never been to India, but you make me feel as if I know the places you describe. I especially like the main character, Javed,  and I feel worried about the fact that here are so few tigers left in the wild. Please write some more books set in exotic places.

From

Tiffany Little

P.S. I plan to be a writer when I'm older. If you have any advice, please reply to me at tiffany.little@hodder.co.uk

I think one of the problems about being a writer is how long you have to hang around waiting for something to happen. Like for instance, you send a book off for it to get published, and no one writes back to you for ages! You're just twiddling your thumbs. Then you get a letter saying, thank you, we liked your story very much, but we can't publish it after all – then you send it off to someone else.

Gorgeous told me this the other day. He said this happened to Emily Brontë when she wrote *Wuthering Heights*, and then it became one of the most famous books ever! It was when we were talking about the short story competition I entered, and he was asking me if I'd heard the result yet. Not yet. Soon. Some time this week. I know I'm not gonna win.

Last night Dad began some major building work on our kitchen. He's hammering away right now, knocking down a wall to make the kitchen bigger.

Bang-bang-bang. It drives Bud crazy. He's acting like an earthquake has happened and he has to take shelter under my bed! He lies there and shakes all over. 'It's OK, Bud,' I tell him. 'The world isn't about to end.' But dogs don't see things the way we do.

So now we've got no gas and no water downstairs. We're eating takeaways. Dad's covered in brick and plaster dust. His eyes are like two little round holes in a white mask.

This is the most exciting thing that's happening in my life right now. We're having a new kitchen. Wow!

Scott is going for the World Telly-Watching Record, and he stands a good chance.

I was wrong! The world as we know it is about to end. Gran Little just arrived. Or should I say the human hurricane?

'Scott, get up from the sofa and say hello to your gran!' She swept in unannounced. A click of the remote and the screen went blank.

'Hey!' big bro protested. 'I was watching that!'

'Give me a hug!' Gran grasped him and squeezed his ribs, then gave me the same treatment. 'I came to supervise while your dad gets on with the kitchen,' she explained. 'And judging by the state of this living-room, it's a good job I did!'

No more slobbing around, leaving shoes in the middle of the floor for Bud to chew. No more crisp packets shoved down the sides of the sofa. No more cold baked beans. Hello proper washes, clean shirts and three course meals.

Never suppose that the lack of a cooker could stop Gran cooking. She brought her own, in the shape of camping gas stoves and canisters.

'The only thing I can't do is bake,' she declared, 'so I brought supplies from home.'

Supplies   =   1 tin choc chip cookies
1 Delia Smith carrot cake
2 doz. scones
1 sponge jam roll
1 tin ginger nuts

All home baked, of course.

'Now, kiddos!' she said, after she'd laid out the goodies. 'I want you to tidy this room of all the magazines and litter. Then one of you has to take Bud for a walk.'

'Scott, it's your turn!' I got in before he could.

''S not.'

''Tis.'

''S not!'

We really behave well with an audience.

'Scott, you do it tonight, and Tiffany will do it in the morning.'

We both sulked. You don't argue with our whirlwind Gran.

She cooked and made Dad stop work for tea.

'How did you know we were living in the middle of a pile of rubble?' he asked. She lives thirty miles away, by the sea.

'A little bird told me.'

'You've been talking to Gina again!' Dad guessed straight off.

'And since when was there a law against talking to my own daughter-in-law?'

The steak and chips smelled good. Bud slavered under the table.

'Gina just happened to mention that Tiff and Scott were due to stay with her over Easter because you'd be busy in the house. She said something about a new kitchen, and I said it was a pity you didn't get around to it before the separation. It might have made all the difference.'

'Thanks for that little show of loyalty, Mum!' Dad tucked in without taking offence. He's used to these digs from Gran.

'Well, you've been promising her a new kitchen for as long as I can remember. A woman likes a nice kitchen.'

She does? This was news to me. I mean, imagine spending your life slaving over a cooker. No way.

'And what's been happening with this teacher you took up with? Carli what's-er-name?'

Uh-oh, touchy subject! Carli Ganeri is my art teacher at school. She's been out with Dad a few times, but he says it's nothing serious. They go to concerts, films and stuff. I don't mind – it's cool to see Dad dressed up and looking cheerful. But Scott hates the sight of her, don't ask me why.

'Carli's fine,' Dad told Gran, concentrating on his steak. End of subject.

No homework tonight, so I fancied some

mindless flicking through back copies of mags. Hot gossip on Madonna and Kylie. Lowdown on the latest soap opera hunks. Quizzes: Are you a techno-phobe?

Question 1 – What's a palmtop?

(a) the top part of a palm tree

(b) a computer that fits in your palm

(c) part of your hand.

Win a super sparkly Boogie Kit with lip-gloss, lip balm and nail polish! Blah-de-blah!!

Blah-blah-de-blah! Horoscopes. Thank your lucky stars!

'Leo chicks are born leaders, but you still need a group of best mates you can rely on. You dress to kill, and adore being the centre of attention. Look at me! is your catchphrase, and don't you just love it!'

No! I wonder if I was born on the cusp, or something, cos I'm definitely not your typical Leo. For instance, when Georgeous asks me a question in class, I curl up and die, even though English is my best subject. And if there's any limelight going around, I'm happy for Ellie to grab it.

Update on the Ellie-Carli-Lisa row: Ellie rang me half an hour ago. We had this conversation with the sound of hammering in the background.

Her: Hey, Tiff. Guess what! I've just been speaking to Carli!

Me: Carli Hewitt?

Her: Yeah.

Me: Did she ring you?'

Her: No, the other way round. I decided I couldn't stand the atmosphere any longer. I mean, the whole band would start to suffer if we let this row get out of hand. So I rang and we had this chat . . .

Me: What did you say?

Her: I said, 'Look, let's sort this out.' And she said, yeah, it was a pretty naff situation, and to be honest, she wasn't the one who'd started it.

Me: Who had?

Her: Lisa. Carli said she dragged her off and started bitching about me the moment Heather announced I was lead singer, saying I was a spoiled cow and all that. Carli only agreed so as to keep her quiet. Really, Carli thinks I deserve to head up the band.

Me: *(in a surprised tone)* She said that?

Her: Yeah, honest. She said sorry about the insult, and that I had real charisma!

(Charisma/kə-riz'mə/n. capacity to inspire followers with devotion and enthusiasm. Divine gift or talent)

Me: *(in a doubtful voice)* That's cool, Ellie.

Her: So tomorrow, Carli and I are gonna blank Lisa. And Carli's coming here to my house tomorrow night to rehearse a few numbers.

Me: How will that make Lisa feel?

Her: Who cares? Carli and I will have to carry her until Heather notices she's not pulling her weight. Then, who knows?

That's Ellie for you. She may be down but she's never out. I reckon she's gonna be Britain's second female prime minister.

Sleeptime. Zzzz . . .

Wednesday, April 3rd

Your stars – *Words of wisdom from a wrinkly relly carry more than a grain of truth. Take her advice and find yourself plonked slap-bang in the middle of a mega opportunity.*

Wrinkly relly = Gran? Dunno.

Cool! Fan-tastic! Unbelievable! I won the short story competition!!!
   I WON THE PRIZE!!!!
The letter came this morning.

Dear Ms Little,
We're pleased to name you as the winner of the
J.L.B Bookstores Young Writers' Competition.
Your entry, *Marie-Nicole*, was judged the best out
of all age groups in the children's category.

We would be very pleased if you could attend the J.L.B award ceremony this Saturday, April 6th, 1.00 p.m. at the Flamingo Hotel, Nelson Street, London. Prizes will be presented by international best-selling author, Adam Acrecliffe. Please bring a friend and an accompanying adult.

Regards,

James L Battison

RSVP

Wow! My heart jumped and skipped, my hands trembled. I WON! *Marie-Nicole* was the best entry out of all the age groups!

Texted Shah, Geri and Ellie:
  Cool news!! Won sht stry comp. Am gonna b
  FAMOUS!
Shah texted me back:
  Congrats! Cn I stll spk 2 u whn u'r
  FAMOUS?!

Ellie said:

Wow! Fnktstic! Am jelus!

Geri replied:

U r a brain-bx, Tff Ltl!

Then I ran and told Gran and Dad.

Dad laughed and said where on earth did I get my talent from? I could tell he was dead pleased.

Gran gave me the biggest hug ever. She shrieked and jumped up and down, asking, 'What's the stort shory about, kiddo?'

'It's about Marie-Nicole, who's mega brave during the French Revolution in 1789. Her dad's a candlemaker and he joins the revolution, but Marie-Nicole has fallen in love with a duke and she risks everything to disguise him and smuggle him away from the guillotine.' I could've told her every word off by heart, practically.

'All the kids of Paris are starving and living on the streets. They soften the heart of the duke, who has to run away into exile. So he sends piles of money for them, via Marie-Nicole, which makes Marie-Nicole's father change his mind about some of the aristocrats. He tells the revolutionaries to stop chopping off heads, and afterwards, when everything's back to normal, he allows the duke and Marie-Nicole to get married.'

'How romantic!' Gran gasped. 'It sounds just like *Les Misérables*!'

I had to put her straight on this little point. 'No, my story's completely different!'

'Oh, it's wonderful!' she beamed. 'Our little Tiffany is going to London to meet Adam Acrecliffe!'

'With a friend and a grown-up!' I reminded them.

'The grown-up had better be your mum,' Dad said. 'You're with her this weekend, so it'd be best for her to take you. She'll enjoy that.'

'And which friend?' Gran asked.

Geri, Ellie or Shah? 'Dunno. Haven't decided. Tell you later. Bye!' I climbed the heap of rubble in the kitchen and scooted out of the house. I couldn't wait to tell Mr Fox and see the look on his face!

☆

30

'Nice one, Tiff,' Georgeous said.

I'd collared him walking along the corridor with Miss Westlake before assembly.

'Congratulations!' Heather added.

'You're my star pupil. I always knew you'd go far.' George grinned at me. His eyes had kind of lit up.

'To London!' Heather sighed. 'Lucky you!'

Mr Fox thought he'd better pull me down to earth, so I didn't float off like a helium balloon.

'But remember what you said in your essay; don't let it go to your head. Keep both feet firmly on the ground. I don't have to tell you that there's a lot of hard work involved in becoming a really good writer, because I know you already realize that.'

I nodded like one of those naff dogs on the back ledge of a car.

'Does this mean you'll miss band practice this weekend?' Heather asked.

I don't sing or play any instruments; I'm her special assistant, taking down notes and stuff. Once I even wrote a song for the band. 'Yeah, sorry!'

'Don't worry. We'll manage for one rehearsal. And, Tiffany, I hope you have a really wonderful day!'

My head did swell up like a pumpkin, I must admit.

The Head announced my news in assembly and I could've died! But at the same time, I felt proud. No one else at the school had ever won a national writing competition, so they were sending a reporter from the local newspaper to interview me. *Moi!* Tiffany Little!

'Hey, Tiff; how much did you win?' Dom Skinner asked during Geography.

'Fifty pounds' worth of book tokens,' I told him.

He wrinkled his nose and snorted. 'Tiddly-skiddly peanuts!'

'It's not about money!' I sniffed.

'Oo-oooh!' Dom and Squealer yodelled. 'Listen to 'er!'

The reporter came during Ma Malone's French lesson.

'You'll have to catch up what you miss over the Easter holiday,' she warned. No, 'Well done, Tiffany,' or anything. Prune-face!

Jon the Journalist took me to the secretary's office and asked me loads of questions – Was English my fave subject? When did I start writing stories? Did I illustrate them? Did I work on a computer?

Then he took pictures of me. First, I had to hold up a book and pretend to be reading. Then he sat me in front of Mrs Skinner's computer and asked me to look as if I was

being creative. After that, he chatted up Mrs Skinner and I had to go back to class.

'When will it be in the paper?' I asked as I sloped off. I felt hot and a bit stupid. What if the photo turned out to be naff? My stupid ears might be sticking out through my hair, or I might have a geeky smile. Nightmare. I went hotter and stickier.

'Friday,' Jon said, without looking at me. He was concentrating on Mrs Skinner's see-through shirt.

The day before I go to London. Please make it a good photo! I prayed, then snuck off to the loo so I didn't have to go back to French before the lunch bell went.

'OK, so what're you gonna wear?' Ellie asked. We were in the queue for hot dinner.

I shook my head. 'Dunno.'

'Oh, Tiff, you've gotta take this seriously! The way you look on Saturday really matters!'

'OK, how should I look?'

'Really cool. Like, intelligent, but not geeky. You need the latest style of top and some fitted trousers. Show a bit of midriff. Pity you don't have your belly-button pierced . . .'

'Wait up!' I told her. 'I'm not sure about bits of me being bare. They're probably all gonna be in suits and stuff.'

'Yeah, boring old . . .' Ellie left a gap and raised her eyebrows. 'Listen, Tiff, I'll lend you one of my tops and my thin pink patent leather belt. What shoes d'you plan to wear?'

'You're so lucky, Tiff!' Shah sighed. We'd collected our fish pie and veg (yuck!) and had sat down in a quiet corner.

'I know it!' London – red buses, black taxis, the river, Big Ben and Madame Tussaud's.

'You can go to Trafalgar Square and feed the pigeons. You can visit Buckingham Palace!'

'Yeah, but the best bit is meeting Adam Acrecliffe,' I sighed. 'I know I'm gonna be really, really nervous!'

'Go on the London Eye!' Geri ordered. 'And come back and tell us what it was like!' We were clearing our plates and chucking cutlery into the bucket, all in one neat, noisy manoeuvre.

'Maybe,' I hedged. I wasn't sure about zooming up in one of those see-through pods, watching the whole of London open up under my feet.

'Go on, don't be chicken! From up there, I bet the city looks like that shot at the beginning of EastEnders – Da-da-da-da-daa-da-daah!'

I grinned. 'Yeah, maybe!'

Yeah, my mates are cool. They're all mega excited for me.

'Tiff, you really, really deserve this,' Shah told me.

'It's like a dream come true!' I admitted.

'I always knew you could do it!' Ellie said.

And Geri called me a rising literary superstar. 'Next thing you know, they'll turn *Marie-Nicole* into a movie, and you'll be schmoozing with the stars!'

Which leaves me with a problem and only two days to decide.

Who – I mean WHO – am I gonna take with me?

Thursday, April 4th

Your stars – *You've been overdoing it lately, and now it's time for others to take care of you. Sleep in late, then chill out with the girls.*

'Put all three names in a hat,' Gran suggested. This was last night, after I'd explained the BIG problem.

'I want to take all three of them – Geri, Ellie and Shah – but the invite says only one. Which means that two people are gonna feel left out, and they've all been really great to me.'

'If you use the hat method, then the choice is made for you. Otherwise, you're never going to make up your mind.' Gran was hoovering for England, yelling above the noise.

So I came upstairs and did the hat thing. I scribbled Shah, Geri and Ellie's names on three pieces of paper, folded them and chucked them into my red furry wool-beret. Then I blindfolded myself with a scarf and scrabbled around inside the hat.

'Dial 999! Tiff's either gone blind or mad!' Scott cried from the door of my room.

'Naff off, Scott!'

'Fetch the strait-jacket, she's dangerous!'

By this time, I'd picked a name and was tearing off my blindfold. I unfolded the paper and read it:

Totally fair. No problem. Ellie would come to London with me and Mum.

So I rang her.

'Wow, Tiff, that'd be really cool!' she sighed.

'But?'

'Well, the thing is, I have to rehearse.'

For the band. 'Yeah, I forgot,' I admitted.

'And this one is really important,' Ellie raced on. 'Y'know how things are with Carli and Lisa;

I have to be there on Saturday and make sure they don't gang up against me again. And it'll be my first rehearsal as lead singer. If I didn't show, it'd be like a football team running on to the pitch without their captain.'

'Yeah, I can see that. Listen, Ellie, it's cool.'

'Can I still help you decide what to wear?' she asked, obviously scared that she'd upset me.

'Course. Come round here tomorrow morning, ten o'clock.'

'Cool. See ya.'

'Yeah, see ya. Bye!'

Shah's was the second name out of the hat.

'Oh Tiff, that'd be amazing!' Shah sighed. 'I'd really, really love to be part of your big day!

'But?' I asked

'But Saturday's the day that Skye comes down from Scotland. I promised Mum and Dad I'd meet her at the station.' She sounded genuinely sad. 'Listen, I'll ask them if I can come with you instead.'

'No, don't.' I remembered how much Skye's visit meant to the whole family. And Skye's cool – we all really like her.

'Go and meet your sister,' I told Shah. 'I can

tell you about my big day when I get back.'

'OK, but I hate it when this happens. Why can't I split myself in two?'

'Hey, no problem. Come round tomorrow at ten. You can help me plan what I'm gonna say to Adam Acrecliffe!'

'Cool, Tiff. See ya.'

'Yeah, see ya. Bye!'

I was pretty stressed out when I rang Geri, the last name out of the hat.

What if no one could come? How sad was that?

'What me?' Geri yelled. 'You're kidding! Wow, me! Come to London? Hey, cool!'

Phew. 'Listen, Mum's taking us. We get the whole day there. In the afternoon we go to a big hotel and I get my prize.'

'Sounds funktastic. I can't wait! Wow, London – you and me, Tiff!'

'Come round tomorrow morning. Let's make plans.'

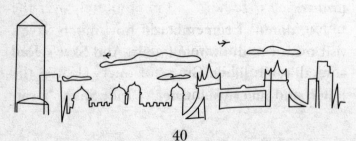

'Definitely The Eye!' Geri insisted. 'If I go to London, I have to see it from the top!'

'Still on Cloud 9?' Gran asked at lunch (macaroni cheese with tomatoes, followed by chunks of carrot cake).

I nodded hard.

Dad had stopped hammering for five minutes to eat his macaroni cheese. 'I'm excited for you, love. It's not every day that something like this happens.'

'Yeah, I wish you could come.'

'Never mind. Your mum can take photos. Hey, I take it you did ring her to tell her?'

I was looking at my lovely dad, all covered in plaster dust, munching his lunch and thinking of others. I nodded again.

'Was she pleased?' Dad asked.

'Big time.'

'Tiffany, that's wonderful!' was what she'd said. 'I'm speechless . . . wait a moment, let me pull myself together . . . I'm absolutely over the moon for you. You're a star!'

'Good. You'll have a great day out.' Dad smiled at me, while Gran, for once, cleared the plates and said nothing.

p.m.

What to wear?

a. silver halter top   b. stripey top   c. pale blue fleece
   black trousers   short skirt   jeans
   black boots   black boots   trainers

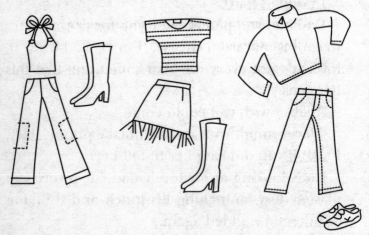

Or, black trousers with stripey top, short skirt with pale blue fleece, jeans with silver halter top?

Make-up — a little or a lot?
Hair — up or down? Spiky or smooth? With or without butterfly clips/hair bobbles/hair slides?

Will wait till tomorrow morning to take advice from fashion guru, Ellie.

God, I've got butterflies going mad in my stomach, even just thinking about Saturday!

Notes for the start of a new story – even better than *Marie-Nicole*.

<u>Main character</u>:
Kaz (~~short for~~ not short for anything)
School dropout
Ran away from home aged 13
Living rough
No friends or family
Skinny, dark-haired, suspicious eyes
<u>Setting</u>:
Dirty city streets
Railway stations, Underground
<u>Storyline</u>:
Kaz is used to life on the streets. He survives by begging, sleeping in squats, hostels and doorways. Big Issue seller, Marti, makes friends with Kaz and learns his background. She begins to persuade him to look up his family. Eventually, Kaz agrees. Marti helps him pick up the trail, but they find big changes back home, and both Marti and Kaz are sucked in to unexpected danger . . .

I need a reason why Kaz ran away in the first place, plus what it is that's dangerous when he eventually goes back. Maybe his cruel step-dad has killed his mum and hidden the body in the yard . . . Anyway, it could be a murder mystery of some sort. I think it could be cool, with a happy ending. No romance between Marti and Kaz though – she's 25 and he's only 16.

I wonder what it's like to write something that everyone wants to read. Like, five million copies in the first year. Scary! TV people would want to interview you, not just the tiddly little local newspaper. You would just have to say your name and everyone would gasp: 'Wow, not THE Tiffany Little, who wrote *Kaz*?!!!'

Bang-bang-bang! Dad sounds like he's breaking through the Berlin Wall (which we learned about in History). Even I think the whole house is gonna fall down, let alone Bud.

The dog races upstairs, throws himself against my door and breaks into the room. Normally he's a black and brown German shepherd with a big pink tongue, but right now he's a ghost-dog, all whitish-grey.

I whisk him out of my room and dump him straight in the bath, where I turn on the shower.

'Stop him!' Dad yells from down below. 'He's covered in cement and sand!'

Uh-oh! Cement! The dust is starting to cake in big lumps on Bud's fur. Soon I'm gonna have a rock-hard, concrete dog! Bud loves the shower and starts to play. Paws up against the white tiles, shaking himself dry . . .

'Down, Bud! Stand still!' I'm sounding desperate as Gran rushes in.

'Oh, kiddo!' She sees the cement splattered everywhere, and Bud bouncing out of the bath, jumping up at her. In a flash she grabs hold of his collar and wraps him in a towel. She rolls him on the floor until he's mainly dry, then lets him stand up.

Bud shakes himself a few more times. This time, a light spray of grey cement hits the tiles.

'He still needs hosing clean in the yard,' Gran decides, lifting this giant dog in her arms and staggering downstairs. Bud is licking her face, expecting a treat.

'Tiffany, you clean up the bathroom while the cement is still wet!'

This takes a whole hour. Honestly, how is a writer supposed to do any work when she lives in a madhouse like mine? By the time I'm finished, it's tea-time. Dad needs the bathroom to take a shower before he goes out with Carli. Gran's made Lancashire hot-pot with dumplings.

'Not bad for a camping-stove effort,' she smiles, 'even if I do say so myself!'

I'm an alien! I wasn't born on the same planet as other girls my age.

Proof: I've just read *Boy Trouble* in my mag.

'Dear Katya,
I'm in love with a cute boy in my year, but he doesn't want to know . . .'

'Dear Katya,
I really fancy a boy at school, and I know he feels the same way too . . .'

'Dear Katya,
For ages I've fancied this boy who used to live
on my street . . .'

'Dear Katya,
I started a new school in September, and since
then I've fancied *two* boys who are friends . . .'

I am; I'm a freak! I've never fancied anyone in my school in my life (except Nic Heron, and he doesn't count because he's fifteen).

And yet here they are, all these Rachels and Amys and Gemmas who fancy the pants off kids in their Maths class.

'Dear Katya,
What's wrong with me? I don't fancy Chucky Gilbert. In fact, the idea of kissing him makes me feel sick.'

'Dear Tiffany,
Yes, I see your problem, and you are unusual, I must admit. Have you thought about closing your eyes when you kiss Chucky? Would this make a difference?'

Nightmare!

Anyway, what's the point? If you fancy someone, and then you fall in love with them, you only end up with the kind of mess Mum and Dad are in.

I said this to Gran after Mum had popped in earlier this evening to rearrange the whole weekend. Gran hugged me and said couples sometimes went through bad patches, but it didn't mean that falling in love in the first place was a bad thing. I'm not convinced.

Mum only called round to see us because she knew Dad was out. She rang up and checked first.

'Where did he go?' she asked me.

'Dunno.'

'Who with?'

'Not sure.' (Which was a lie.)

'Will he be long?' she fired questions like a machine-gun, *ack-ack-ack*!

'Dunno.'

'Is your gran there?'

'Yep, hang on.'

Then she and Gran arranged the visit. Gran had a cup of tea and home-made biscuits ready for Mum when she arrived.

'Oh my god!' Mum said, when she saw the hole that used to be the kitchen. 'It looks like a bomb-site!'

'Tell me!' Gran laughed. 'But you know Ross; he'll do a good job.'

'If he ever finishes it,' Mum said sharply. Then she saw Scott hovering at the top of the stairs. 'Hey, Scott. How was the first day of freedom?' Meaning, Easter hols.

Scott grunted.

'I expect you're doing loads of revision for GCSEs!'

' – NOT!'

'That's my boy!'

Weird, but the way Mum used to tease Scott when she lived with us just isn't funny any more. He doesn't think so either, to judge by the way he slammed his door.

'Don't worry, it's a touch of jealousy,' Gran told Mum. 'Now that Tiffany's won this writing competition, poor Scott's nose has been put way out of joint.'

I don't think so, Gran. I don't think that's it at all.

Neither did Mum. She'd breezed in, all bright and cheerful in her new lilac work suit and smooth haircut, until she saw the bomb site and got up Scott's nose. Then she went quiet and hurt.

I followed her and Gran into the living-room.

'So, Tiff, what time do we have to set off on

Saturday?' Mum asked, just managing a smile.

'Can we get an early train and go sight-seeing?'

She nodded. 'Sounds great.'

'Geri wants to go on The Eye.'

'Oh, I don't know about that. Don't you have to book seats weeks in advance?'

I pulled a face. 'Maybe.'

'Let me phone and find out.' Mum had drunk her tea and sunk back into her chair. Even her new hairdo didn't hide the fact that she looked dead tired.

'Why not give your mum a rest and make your plans tomorrow?' Gran said quietly.

I felt like a pricked balloon, losing all its air.

'Tomorrow!' Gran insisted, jerking her head toward the door. I took the hint and left. Bud charged up to me, asking for a walk, but I couldn't be bothered. Instead, I went up to my room.

A weird thing has happened since Dad started pulling down walls in the kitchen. There's now a gap in the ceiling, and just my bedroom floorboards between me and down-stairs, which means I can hear every word anyone says.

' . . . I understand what you're going through, Gina,' Gran was murmuring. 'I honestly do.'

'How can you?' Mum sighed. 'You and Stephen were happily married for thirty-eight years!'

'Married, yes. But let me tell you, life wasn't always a bed of roses with Steve, God bless him. In fact, there was many a time when I could've walked away.'

I heard Mum gasp. 'I never knew that! Ross never told me.'

'Ross doesn't know. In those days, we didn't let on to the kids. And the fact is, Steve and me got through the hard times, regardless.'

There was a long silence, except for tea-cups in saucers. I sat cross-legged on my bed, soaking it all in.

'So, kiddo, any regrets?' Gran asked softly.

'Hundreds,' Mum sighed. 'Mostly about Scott and Tiff. I miss them every minute of the day.'

Suddenly my heart stopped, my throat went narrow and I had hot tears in my eyes.

'What about Ross?'

'Of course, I miss him too. Sometimes I turn around and have to bite my tongue to stop myself from calling Neil "Ross".'

Gran kept quiet.

'Force of habit,' Mum laughed. Not a happy laugh. 'You won't tell Ross I said that, will you?'

'It won't go beyond this room!' Gran promised.

Hah! I sat on my bed sniffing, with the sound coming through the floorboards clear as anything.

'You've been very good to me since the separation,' Mum told Gran. 'And really I don't deserve it.'

Meaning, she was the one who left. She was the one who found smarmy Neil.

'Gina, I'm very fond of you,' Gran said in a husky voice. 'And I want you to know, just so that you're never in any doubt; you'll always be family to me!'

Friday, April 5th

***Your stars** – You'll soon be going to lots of parties and they could hold the key to romance. So dress up and boogie!*

This is my pic in the paper!

LOCAL GIRL WINS PRIZE

Sad, or what.

Yep, it's those ears again. I may as well pack my trunk (elephant ears … trunk, ha ha!) and join the freaks in the circus.

And this is the article:

LOCAL GIRL WINS PRIZE

11 year old Ashbrook schoolgirl, Tiffany Little, has beaten off rivals to win a major writing competition. Tiffany travels to London this weekend to collect her prize from international bestselling author, Adam Acrecliffe. School spokesperson, George Fox, says that Ashbrook Comprehensive is proud of their star pupil's achievement. He believes that talented Tiffany's future looks bright.

The piece is tucked away on page 7, just before the classified ads.

Dad went out early to buy the paper, brought it in and slapped it down on the table grinning from ear to ear.

Scott laughed at the photo, so I socked him.

Gran broke us up, then read every word at

least three times – '11 year old Tiffany . . . major writing competition . . . international bestselling author . . . proud of their star pupil . . . Tiffany's future looks bright!'

She sat down with a big sigh, shaking her head as if she couldn't believe what she'd just read.

Like Dad, I had an idiot grin on my face. I never thought that success at writing could feel this good. I've dreamed about it hundreds of times – pictured my books on bookshop shelves, seen myself signing autographs, imagined blockbuster movies 'based on the book by Tiffany Little'.

But the dreams were nothing like as good as the way it actually feels – like a bubble of happiness inside, making me smile and every bit of me glow!

'Hey, Tiff, can we still speak to you?' Geri was the first to arrive at my house. She'd seen the photo and the article, and so had everyone else at home. 'Mum's well impressed.'

I went bright red, as if the inner glow just got stronger.

'She's going around showing everyone the paper, saying, "That's my daughter's best friend. Geri is going along to the award ceremony with her.'"

I got the shakes a bit when Geri said the word, 'ceremony'. My legs went weak as I pictured walking through a crowd, up on to a platform to shake hands with A.A.

'What if I trip up the steps?' I gasped.

'You won't!' Geri had won plenty of prizes herself – for tennis, hockey, netball and akido, you name it . . .

'Will you make sure that I do it right?' I pleaded.

Geri grinned and nodded.

'Oh my God, look at the picture!' Ellie came in waving the newspaper. 'Is he a naff photographer, or what?'

OK, OK, Ellie, don't rub it in!

'They always do that; they make you look like a moron! It happened to me when I won that disco dancing contest when we were 8, remember? I mean, Tiff, you look much better than this in real life!'

I looked again. Yep, I've got a stupid fake smile and my eyes are half-shut. The inner bubble is getting smaller.

Then Shah showed up. She glowed like me. I got a big hug and the warmest of smiles. 'Wow, Tiff, this is cool!' was all she said.

Then the BIG QUESTION of what to wear.

Ellie had brought half her wardrobe with her. She flung everything on the bed. Tops with logos like 'Michigan 22 USA' and 'Blabbermouth'. Hipster belts of every colour. Red bandanas and white bandanas with paisley patterns, chunky silver jewellery and a mid-calf fru-fru skirt made of black net.

'Or these!' she drew a pair of bootleg cords out of her bag. 'Corduroy's cool right now.'

I tried them on, but yeah – they made my bum look BIG!

'How about the skirt?' Shah held the black net frilly thing against me.

I could see Shah or Ellie in it, but not me, so I shook my head. 'I have to walk round London first, remember.'

'Yeah, but I think you should look cute.' Even Geri was encouraging me to choose something spesh. 'How about the skirt with a plain white top?'

'What about shoes?'

'These!' Ellie dug into the bottomless bag and held up a pair of black trainers with white stripes. 'That'd be funktasic! A real party skirt and cool trainers – like a weird caj-glamour mix of styles, with your hair smooth at the front and spiky at the back. And like Geri says, a plain white sleeveless top, and for outside, you can borrow my black leather jacket with the zips!'

'Try it!' Shah said.

So I did, and y'know what – it looked cool!

'You need millions of black and white bracelets,' Ellie decided while Shah was experimenting with my hair. And yeah, she had them in the bag!

Half an hour later, I was ready for an outside opinion.

'Tiffany's gran!' Geri yelled from the top of the stairs. 'Can you come and look?'

Bang-bang! Dad was hard at work in the bomb-site.

The stairs creaked as Gran made her way up. She took one look and her eyebrows shot up. 'Very nice,' she said in a quivery voice.

'She didn't like it!' Shah hissed as Gran disappeared back downstairs.

'Which means it's cool!' Ellie insisted. 'Honestly, Tiff, it'll crack 'em up!'

I took a deep breath and one more look in the mirror. 'OK, I'll go for it,' I agreed.

'Hey, Tiff's gonna pull a lush lad in London!' Geri cried. Which led to an insult contest, interrupted by hot chocolate and cookies from Gran.

'Walk me through it!' I begged, after we'd polished off the cookies and I'd got changed into my combats and sweatshirt.

'You wanna rehearse the ceremony?' Shah checked.

'Yeah. Then I can work out which hand to use for what.' I was still having kittens about meeting the celebs and receiving the prize.

'OK, I'll be Adam Acrecliffe!' Shah volunteered.

'And I'll be the announcer!' Ellie offered.

'And I'll be me,' Geri said.

So we used the landing, which has three steps up in the middle. Geri and I sat in the bathroom, waiting for Ellie to announce the winner from the higher level, where Shah aka Adam Acrecliffe was waiting.

'And now it gives me special pleasure to announce the overall winner of the junior

writer's section!' Using my hairbrush as a microphone, Ellie talked it up like crazy. 'This is a young lady whose talents amazed our judges. A girl of superb intelligence and insight – truly one in a million. Ladies and gentlemen, would you please give it up for Mi-iss Ti-iffany Li-ittle!'

Geri clapped maniacally, while Shah stood smiling on the platform.

My stomach churned like a cement mixer.

'Go!' Geri gave me a shove along the landing.

Wibble-wobble, my legs turned to jelly. I staggered up the three steps, seeing Shah with a piece of paper in one hand, and the other hand stretched out for me to shake.

'Congratulations, Tiffany,' she said in a deep voice.

I took the paper with my right hand and

offered to shake with my left. Wrong!!! I fumbled and dropped the paper, and as I picked it up, a hair bobble fell out. I came up lop-sided, with half my hair in my face.

'See!' I wailed. This was the kind of disaster I was dreading.

'Again!' Ellie sighed. 'From the top, one more time!'

p.m. A new, slow song for Ellie:

THE COLOURS OF LOVE

> *The sky is misty blue*
> *When I think of you*
> *Blue is my heart*
> *When we're apart*
>
> *The colours of love*
> *Are a rainbow*
> *Rainbow, rainbow . . .*
>
> *The sun is molten gold*
> *When it's you I hold*
> *Yellow the ring*
> *To you I bring*
>
> *The colours of love*
> *Are a rainbow*
> *Rainbow, rainbow . . .*

Now I need a red verse – crimson, scarlet . . .

Will finish it later. Shah has promised Ellie to write some smoochy music to go with the words.

p.m. later.

Better keep the song on hold. I just had a text message from Ellie:

Mjor dsastr – Lisa wlkd out. Gmni cd fold!!!

I rang her straight back. 'What happened?'

'Oh, Tiff, it's pants! Lisa went and told Heather that she wouldn't be in the band if I was lead singer.'

'When?'

'This morning. Heather got a phone call at home from Lisa's mum, saying Lisa couldn't make it to rehearsal tomorrow. Heather got the feeling that something serious was up, and eventually Mrs Sharman told her that she couldn't do a thing with Lisa and that Lisa wanted to quit Gemini because she couldn't stand me!'

'No!'

'Yes, honest.'

'Silly cow!' I was really mad with Lisa-Stupid-Sharman. This band meant a heck of a lot to Ellie and everyone else involved with it.

'I know. But that's what she's doing, and spreading the rumour that I boss everyone

65

around and won't listen to anyone else . . . '

'Don't worry, Heather won't believe that. She sees what happens at rehearsals.' OK, so Ellie has a BIG personality, but she doesn't throw her weight around. All this was just Lisa being jealous. 'So anyway, what did Heather say?'

'She rang around everyone, explaining that Lisa wanted to quit. Apparently Carli already knew, and she didn't even tell me, the back-stabbing little . . . !'

'How about the boys?'

'Callum and Dom think it'll all blow over, and Lisa will be back. Marc never liked Lisa anyway, and says that if she messes us around she shouldn't be *allowed* to come back.'

Messy! 'What did you all decide?'

'To go ahead with the rehearsal. And Heather is willing to give Lisa another chance. But Tiff, if Lisa does show up tomorrow, I can't face her, knowing what she's been saying about me!'

'Yeah, and I don't blame you. But listen, Ellie, you can't let Lisa Sharman push you out of the band. Think about it; that'd be like letting her win!'

'But she must really hate me . . . !' Ellie's voice was breaking down – I had to zoom to the rescue.

'That's *her* problem, OK! It's nothing to do with you, except maybe the fact that you can actually sing and dance better than her. That's what she can't stand. So she sets out to wreck the whole band, and you can't let her do that. No, you have tough it out, Ell!'

'You're right,' she said after a long pause. 'Thanks, Tiff.'

'Just go to the rehearsal and sing better than ever.'

'Yeah, I will.'

'And text me after rehearsal tomorrow. I'll probably be on the train.'

Cool. Hey, and good luck with the celebs!'

'Thanks. I'll need it.'

'Chill out. Enjoy!' she instructed. 'Speak to you later.'

'Don't write any music.' I phoned Shah and filled her in. 'Gemini is in trouble. It might fold.'

'Just what we needed,' Shah sighed.

'Why, what's wrong?' Straight away I was worried; you never heard Shah sounding down, like she did right now.

'Mum and Dad got a letter from school this morning. It was from Mr Geography White.'

'Saying what?' Geography White was joint-Head of Year 7 with Miss Hornby, so it sounded like trouble.

'That Mr Maths White was concerned about my so-called lack of progress in Maths, and Mr Geography White had been asked to write a formal letter, warning that I'd be put down to the bottom set if I didn't watch out.'

'Bummer!' I breathed.

'Yeah, Happy Easter!'

'What did your mum and dad say?'

'Mum went out and bought me a Key Stage 3 maths book. I have to work through it during the holiday.'

'Double-bummer! Listen, Shah, everyone knows that Maths White is a lousy teacher.' Tiff to the rescue again! 'He couldn't teach a . . .

well, he couldn't teach a dolphin to swim!'

Shah almost laughed. 'No, it's me,' she admitted. 'Numbers and me don't get on – y'know, all those equations and angles and things.'

'OK, so we'll help,' I told her. 'Geri, Ellie and me will teach you, starting Monday.'

'Hey, listen to me moaning on! How're you feeling about tomorrow, Tiff?'

'D-d-d-don't mention it!'

'Like that, huh?'

Yeah, sick to the pit of my stomach. Dry mouth, clammy hands, wobbly legs – already! 'Wish me luck,' I stammered.

'You'll be cool!' Shah said. 'Hey, listen; text me and tell me about it, OK?'

'Will do. See you later, OK!'

8.30 p.m.

Mrs Shapiro rang and I picked up the phone.

'Tiffany dear, I'm afraid I have some bad news.'

I froze. Something to do with Geri . . .

'Geri's had an accident.'

'What happened? Is she OK?'

'She fell from a practice wall during her

69

rock-climbing lesson this afternoon. She broke her arm.'

Ouch! I could see her clinging to the wall, losing her footing, plummeting down . . .

'Tiffany, are you there?'

'Yes. How is she?'

'She's fine now that she's been to hospital to have it set. It's a complex fracture of the elbow joint, so they had to put a pin in to hold it in place, then they covered it from wrist to elbow in a plaster cast.'

'So she won't be able to come to London tomorrow?' I asked. How much bad news could a person hear in one evening?

'No dear, that's why I'm ringing.' Mrs Shapiro sounded genuinely sorry. 'Of course, Geri is clamouring still to go with you, but her father and I have said no. She's suffering from shock after a fall like that, so we want her to have a quiet weekend – no visitors, just complete rest.'

I said I understood in a flat voice.

'We really are upset for Geri. It would have been a lovely day for you both.'

'I'm sorry too.' No London Eye. Geri had been mega excited about that.

'But you go ahead and have a wonderful time, Tiff. You and your mum.'

'I will, thanks.'

'And Geri will be thinking of you when you get your prize.'

Thanks again. 'I'll text her after the ceremony,' I promised.

So it's just me and Mum. Me, Mum and the world of celebrity writers!

Saturday, April 6th

Your stars – *You seem so darned confident that sometimes mates forget that you have a big squishy heart. Don't let them trample all over it, otherwise your life will be in knots that will drive you loop-de-loop!*

Didn't sleep. Got up at 6.00 a.m. Train is at half-past nine.

Can't eat breakfast. Keep looking at clothes lying on bed. The black net skirt worries me.

Had a shower, washed my hair. Mum rang to arrange to pick me up at half-eight. Dried my hair and it wouldn't go right. Major panic about bits sticking out that aren't supposed to. Used de-tangler and gel. OK in the end.

Have chickened out of wearing the skirt. Black trousers with a red top, plus boots and a jacket instead. I'm not Geri Halliwell; I'm me!

Saw Scott on his way to the bathroom, and he grunted 'Good luck.' A-Mazing!

Gran keeps offering to make me a packed lunch.

Me : It's OK, Gran. We get lunch there.

Gran: At the hotel? But it's a long time till then. Don't you think you'd better have some thing to be going on with?

Me: No, honest, it's OK!

Gran: Oh, go on. You never know when you'll start feeling peckish.

Me: Gran, don't bother!

Gran: Nonsense kiddo, it's no bother. I'll just pack some cheese and pickle sarnies and a couple of chocolate chip cookies.

Dad grinned and shrugged. He's had a lifetime of Gran's packed lunches. They weigh a ton and contain ten thousand calories.

So she's happy chopping, slicing and buttering, cramming and stuffing fillings between slices of bread.

The queasy feeling in my stomach is getting worse.

Got dressed in outfit. Am happy with trousers. Applied blusher, eye shadow, mascara and lip-gloss. Did hair in sections, with silver scrunchies.

Saw myself from all angles by holding hand mirror and looking at back view in bathroom mirror.

Dad took a photo.

Later: On train with Mum.

She arrived at the house on time, dressed in pale lilac suit. Knee-length hem, fitted jacket with darker purple lapels and pockets. She's had her hair cut in a trendy style, with feathery bits at the side.

Dad and Gran waved us off. ('Don't forget your packed lunches!') We got stuck in a roadworks traffic jam on our way to the station. Sat there for ages, stomach playing up even worse than before.

'Take deep breaths,' Mum told me. 'And don't worry, we'll get there!'

Yeah, at a snail-crawl! Red-amber-green. Green-red. Red-amber . . .

Oh and it was raining and blowing a gale.

Got to station with ten minutes to spare. Parked in multi-storey and sprinted for the intercity. Train sat at the platform until ten to ten, just shuddering every now and then.

'See, we needn't have hurried!' Mum gasped. I spent the time keeping diary up to date, hand shaking like a leaf.

Train finally left at five past ten. 'We're sorry for the delay on this intercity express to King's Cross. This has been due to engineering work on a branch line south of Newark. New estimated time of arrival at King's Cross is twelve-thirty.'

'Bang goes our sightseeing!' Mum sighed.

We have to be at The Flamingo by one o'clock.

'We'd better take the Underground straight to the hotel,' she decided. 'I wouldn't even rely on a taxi getting through the London traffic on time!'

I've been silent since I flopped into my seat,

Coach D, seat 24F. I can feel the coach swaying and clicking over the rails, hear the rain driving against the windows, see the long distance views of fields, rivers and black and white cows. There are patches of blue between the clouds.

'OK?' Mum keeps asking. She's sitting opposite, facing backwards to the way we're going. She looks cool.

I nod and scribble – it's a good way to pass the time. But hey, this writing is wonky! Click, rattle and roll.

More cows and blue sky. Daffodils on the banking.

Towns now. Tiny houses with conservatories and high fences.

Kids playing football on recreation grounds. *Click-click-I'll get-you-there!*

Bigger houses backing on to the railway line. Factories with huge car parks. Spray-graffiti on concrete walls – cool!

'OK?' Mum asks.

I nod.

'The train will shortly be arriving at King's

Cross. GNER thanks you for travelling with us, and please remember to collect all items of luggage before you leave the carriage.'

'Let's go,' Mum says.

Evening: on the train home.

How cool was that!

A-Mazing, funktastic, hard-core, solid!!!

Words don't cover it for the first time ever.

We did the Underground thing, like Mum planned. Down the escalators at King's Cross, on the Victoria Line to Oxford Circus, up again to Regent Street. 'Mind the Gap!' Cool posters of films, buskers with guitars, drums, saxophones.

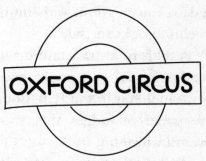

Up the escalators to find Nelson Street (longer than we thought). Running by this time to make The Flamingo before the one o'clock deadline.

Big shops, massive glass office blocks, hotels with doormen in grey uniforms and black top hats. Nose-to-tail traffic, big red buses.

The Flamingo turned out to be super-cool – wood and steel and glass everywhere in Reception, and a notice pointing to the JLB Award Ceremony, 3rd Floor, Acanthus Conference Suite. We went up in the lift, checking our hair in the shiny walls and dabbing on fresh lip-gloss.

'Ready?' Mum said, as the lift jolted to a stop.

We had to tell our names to a woman behind a desk. She gave us name badges and someone else showed us into a room with mountains of Adam Acrecliffe books for sale.

'Tiffany!' A man in a suit came up to me and read my badge. 'Glad you could make it. I'm Sean Miller, chief buyer for JLB Bookstores. I was on the panel of judges that voted *Marie-Nicole* as overall winner!'

He kind of steered us around the books and introduced us to James L. Battison.

JLB was small, bald and wearing a bright blue tie. He offered Mum a glass of red wine. 'Tiffany's writing shows real promise,' he told her. 'I look forward to stocking her first bestseller in the not too distant future!'

The boss of JLB Bookstores had to practically shout above the other voices in the room.

Then Sean swept us on to meet Adam Acrecliffe.

Adam was sitting at a table, signing books. We jumped the queue and Sean handed me a hardback copy of Adam's latest novel, *Underworld*. 'This is Tiffany Little, the overall winner,' he said in a loud voice, which made everyone in the queue stare at me.

So I was keeping tight hold of *Underworld*, trembling from head to foot. Nothing worked – my jaw was locked, my ribs were crushing my lungs and I could hardly breathe.

Adam looked up at me. He's about thirty, with dark, gelled hair and a deep stare. A bit stubbly. Dressed in a black T-shirt and black leather jacket. No suit. 'Nice work,' he grinned, then held out a hand for the book.

'Tiff!' Mum dug me in the ribs.

I jumped and handed over my copy. I watched him write a message:

> 'To Tiff,
> A fellow writer.
> Best wishes,
> Adam Acrecliffe

I swallowed hard and managed a croaky 'Thanks.'

'See you later,' Adam said, then went on signing.

Weird; once I'd done that, I wasn't the least bit nervous!

Sean showed us through to a room with food, and I ate. I had boat-shaped pastry things with tomato and cheese, samosas, fishy things and

vegetables fried in batter. My stomach felt fine.

'Isn't this great?' Mum said, already on to her second glass of wine.

'Isn't he cool?' I whispered, meaning Adam. More like a premiership footballer than how you imagine a writer. I studied his handwriting in the front of my book – big and scrawly, like he'd signed a million times.

'Ladies and gentlemen, could you please work your way through to the main conference room!' a woman announced.

So Mum and I shuffled through into a room with rows of seats and a table at the front. No stage and no steps to trip up, so I was safe.

There were other kids too, I noticed for the first time. A couple were younger than me, but most were older – boys and girls with their best mates and parents.

There were more posters on the walls of the front cover of *Underworld* – a blurred image of wet city streets at night, lit by pink neon, plus big black and white portraits of Adam.

After we'd filed in and sat down, JLB walked to the front with the celeb guest. He made a little speech:

'Kids today get a bad name, but we're here to

celebrate raw talent and achievement, *blah-blah*! Nationwide competition . . . terrifically high standard . . . original imagination, bags of creative energy . . . a credit to the 21st century.'

Mum clapped hard, sitting on the edge of her seat, enjoying every second.

James L sat down and Adam stood up. Not one for speeches, just glad to see that kids were still involved with writing and that the Computer hadn't killed their interest in Books. He told a story about how he'd queued for Quentin Tarantino's autograph when he, Adam, was an unknown, and Tarantino had said, 'Go for it!' when Adam had told him that he wanted to write novels.

'You need the spark that fires your imagination,' he told us. 'And those three words from the great movie maker did it for me. I never looked back!'

We all clapped, then he gave out the prizes. A prize for the Best Under 9 category, then for the Best Under 12 and Best Under 16. Kids went forward to shake hands.

'And the Best Overall Winner is Tiffany Little!' Sean announced.

It was My Big Moment.

I got up and walked like I was on air, straight down the central aisle. I took in every detail; the table, JLB beaming at me, his bald head twinkling under the lights. The firm feel of Adam Acrecliffe's handshake, his nice white teeth and friendly smile.

'Don't look back!' he told me. His magic three words to me!

I grinned, turned and floated back to my seat.

Sunday, April 7th

Your stars *– Thrills and spills are on the cards for Leos this week. Look for your destiny in a Britney lyric!*

Don't-look-back! Don't-look-back! the train wheels told me, all the way home.

Mum and me had done a quick whisk around London on an open-top double-decker bus. We'd seen the Tower, Nelson's Column, the Eye and Buckingham Palace, not in that order. My head was still a whirl of handshakes and congratulations, Mum giggling over her third glass of wine, Sean Miller looking after us and Adam being a celeb in the far corner of the room. Eventually we'd left the award ceremony and done the bus. We'd made it to King's Cross just in time for the 5.30 p.m. train.

Mega moments:
* Having my copy of Underworld signed
* Shaking Adam's hand
* Being clapped by 200 people
* Mum taking a picture of me between Adam and JLB
* Riding in a glass lift on the outside of The Flamingo building
* Giggling with Mum on top of the bus

I texted Geri, Ellie and Shah as we pulled out of London:

Hve died & gon 2 Heavn!!!

They texted me back:

Cool! – Geri
Lucky u! – Ellie
Hey, babe! Glad yor spesh day was cool!
     – Shah

Mum talked a lot on the journey and nearly cried when we pulled into our final destination.

'Tiff, this has been absolutely wonderful!' she told me. 'I'm so proud of you!'

'If you blub, I will too!' I warned her.

We *both* blubbed, as we dived for the multi-storey to pick up her car.

'It must be here somewhere,' Mum sighed. 'Which level did we leave it on?'

'Dunno.' I'd been too uptight earlier in the day to notice.

We had to traipse up and down the concrete stairs, until we spotted a lonely little silver Ka parked in the distance.

I've never been so tired. My brain felt like it was rattling around inside my skull, my eyes wouldn't stay open on the car journey from the station.

'*Don't-look-back! Don't-look-back!*' The rhythm of the train played on inside my head.

'Here we are!' Mum announced at half-nine.

She came in the house for once, and let Scott transfer the photos she'd taken from her digital camera on to his computer screen.

'That's the outside of The Flamingo,' she explained. Then, 'This is the reception area, and that's Tiff talking to James Battison. Look, she's almost as tall as he is!'

Dad and Gran oohed and aahed.

'This is Tiff going up to receive her prize, and

that's her posing between Adam and James.'

'Ooh, first-name terms!' Gran teased.

'Didn't she look lovely?' Mum asked Dad. 'So grown-up!'

I was mega embarrassed. I had a big, idiotic grin on my face in every single photo, but at least my ears were behaving themselves!

We all had hot chocolate in the bomb-site, then Dad and I saw Mum to the front door. 'How much do I owe you for Tiff's train fare?' he asked, putting his hand into his pocket.

'Nothing. My treat.' Mum was tired too by this time. Tired and emotional. Her bottom lip quivered. 'Like your dad said, Tiff, I don't know where you get your talent from, I really don't!'

'Hey, watch it!' Dad grinned. 'Anyway, you both had a great day, that's the main thing.'

'Yeah, I needed a pick-me-up,' Mum admitted. Dad and I waited for more.

'Nothing, forget it.' She went red and the tears welled up.

'What's wrong?' Dad asked.

Mum was opening her car door and climbing in. 'Oh, it's just that Neil and I have decided to split up.'

Bombshell! Emotional fall-out. Run for shelter!

'For good?' Dad asked.

Mum nodded. 'Last Wednesday. It's OK. It was a mutual decision. Things just didn't work out. Sorry, shouldn't have mentioned it on Tiff's big day. Listen, forget it. Bye!'

Voom-voom! – the little Ka sped off down the street.

ALONE AGAIN

One cup on the hook, one raincoat on the door,
One key in the lock, I don't love you any more.

There's a space on the sofa, a crack in my heart,
A blank for my future, now that we're torn apart.

How did this happen, after all the things we said?
The taste of dust and ashes, now that love is dead.

One pillow not slept on, one ring never worn,
Alone again, as helpless as the day that I was born.

OK, so Neil was Mr Smarm, and I for one am not gonna miss him. But I can still imagine how Mum feels!

Later.

Everyone's quiet today. No one's talking. Not even Gran.

Then Ellie drops by and breaks the silence.

'Hey, how was the rehearsal?' I asked.

'Hey, how was your big day?' Ellie began at the same time.

Then we went up to my room for a record

talkathon – rabbit-rabbit-rabbit!

Lisa-this, Lisa-that.

Adam-said-this, Adam-said-that.

'She didn't! She did!'

'He looks cool – nice teeth, funky hair.'

Ellie gabbled on. 'Lisa told Carli not to speak to me, and Heather overheard and said that if Lisa behaved like that one more time, she was out of the band for good. That soon shut Lisa up!'

I wasn't listening. 'Adam signed his latest book. Look at his groovy handwriting. He said, "Don't look back!"'

'Lisa still had a mega-strop, but we ignored her. We learned a new song.'

'Adam's even more of a hunk in real life than he is in this photo. He's got a website with every-thing about his life and career.'

'Girls, didn't you hear the doorbell? Fuchsia's here!' Gran interrupted.

Shah came in; smiles all round. 'How cool is this!'

'What?' we asked.

'You two; me. We're all happy.'

'Did Skye get here?' I asked.

Shah nodded. 'She brought her boyfriend,

Callum. It looks like lurve!'

We quizzed Shah about Callum. Tall, thin, number 2 haircut, mouth like Matt Damon, eyes like Brad Pitt. We gave our approval.

'Hey, let's go visit Geri,' Shah suggested. She dived into her rucksack and pulled out a chocolate buttons Easter Egg.

'I brought her this.'

Choccy is Geri's favourite food, so we bought two more eggs on the way. A Mars Bar one from me, and Quality Street from Ellie. Mrs Shapiro opened the door.

'Who is it?' Geri yelled from the telly room.

'Da-dah!' We burst in on her, bearing eggs.

'Funktastic!' she sighed. She showed us her sling and we signed her plaster cast.

To Geri,
No more climbing walls!
luv, Shah xxx

To Action Girl
Funk it up, Babe!
luv, Ellie x

To Geri,
Don't look down!
luv, Tiff
xxxxxxxxx

Then we filled her in on all our Saturdays.

'And I was stuck in watching lousy telly,' she moaned.

'D'you wanna see my personal message from Adam?' I asked, showing her my precious copy of *Underworld*.

We all read it together:

> 'To Tiff,
> A fellow writer.
> Best wishes,
> Adam Acrecliffe.

'Yeah!' they all sighed. 'Tiff and Adam Acrecliffe. How cool is that!'

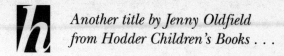

*Another title by Jenny Oldfield
from Hodder Children's Books . . .*

Definitely Daisy 1
You're a disgrace, Daisy!

Meet Daisy Morelli – a magnet
for trouble and a master plotter.
When things go wrong – and they
always do – who gets the blame?
Definitely Daisy!

Daisy's fed up with school, so
she plans to run away – chucking
in boring lessons for footballing
stardom! If only the junior
Soccer Academy will have her . . .